HAROLD'S CIRCUS

HAROLD'S CIRCUS

by Crockett Johnson

ISBN 0-590-31902-7

12 11 10 9 8 7 6 5 4 3 2   6 7 8 9/8 01 2/9

Printed in the U.S.A.   11

SCHOLASTIC INC.

New York Toronto London Auckland Sydney

One moonlit evening, mainly to prove to himself he could do it, Harold went for a walk on a tightrope.

He made sure the rope was drawn tight
and straight, so it wouldn't sway.

He skipped lightly across it, finding it fun to be a tightrope walker, high up over the rest of the circus.

He stayed up on the rope with the greatest
of ease, until he lost his balance.

It also is easy to fall off a tightrope.

Harold fell, twisting and turning, with
his purple crayon tight in his hand.

By a stroke of luck, a comfortable-looking
curve appeared beneath him.

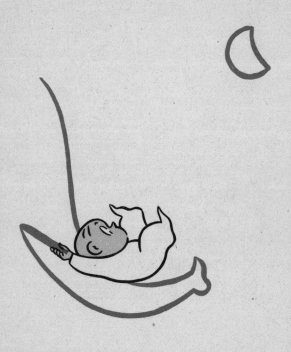

And he landed on an elephant's trunk.

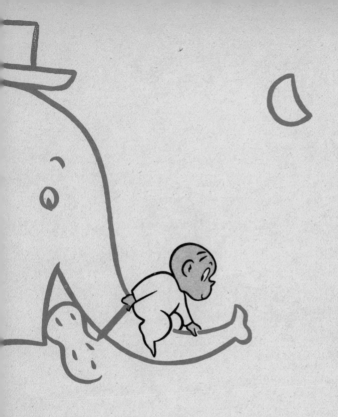

Quite a trick, he thought, as he rewarded
the elephant with a large peanut.

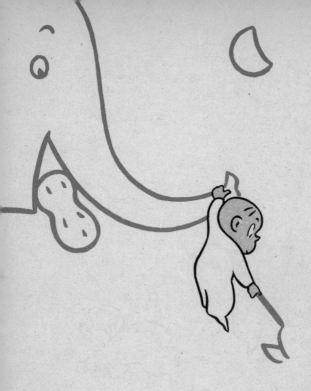

Elephants are such tall animals. Harold
was still a long way from the ground.

So he swung down from the elephant's
trunk to the neck of a smaller animal.

It was a lovely circus horse, beautifully trained, and Harold easily put him into a brisk trot.

Harold rode with no saddle, in a splendid exhibition of circus riding.

At the finish of his bareback act he leapt
gracefully from the horse.

To his embarrassment, he fell and turned
a rather ridiculous somersault.

Before anyone could laugh at the mishap
Harold pretended he had been clowning.

He quickly put on a clown's hat.

He put a clown's smile on his face. And
he acted silly, like a clown.

Finally he took off the hat and the smile.

And he gave them back to the clown.

The real clown was extremely funny. And
Harold laughed and laughed at him.

This, Harold told himself, probably was
the best circus he had ever seen in his life.

Like all circuses, it had a fat lady.

She was really amazingly fat.

And, of course, there was a very tall man.

He was really astoundingly tall.

And next to him was a very small man.

There was another man, a lemonade man.

He had a great tank of lemonade.

Harold stopped for a drink of it, through
a straw. It was quite refreshing.

He left some money on the counter to pay
for the drink and he went on, looking for
the man who is shot out of a cannon.

Harold wasn't sure what a man who is shot out of a cannon would look like.

But, anyway, he wasn't there, though the
cannon was nearly ready.

A circus can't wait. There was only one thing to do.

The cannon fitted Harold perfectly.

He got into it.

And he shot out of it.

He went up fast.

He sailed to the top of the circus, where the trapezes are, and the flying rings.

He reached out.

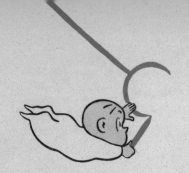

He caught on to a flying ring.

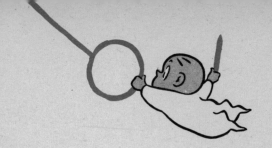

He swung far out on it.

He let go, doing a startling flip-flop in
the air, and he dived straight down.

He was sure the elephant would be there
to catch him again.

Once more, a reassuring curve appeared
beneath him.

But he landed surprisingly hard. This was no elephant's trunk.

It was the tail of a lion. Somehow a lion
had gotten loose in the circus.

Before anyone could quite recognize the
danger and become alarmed, Harold was
at work getting the lion into a cage.

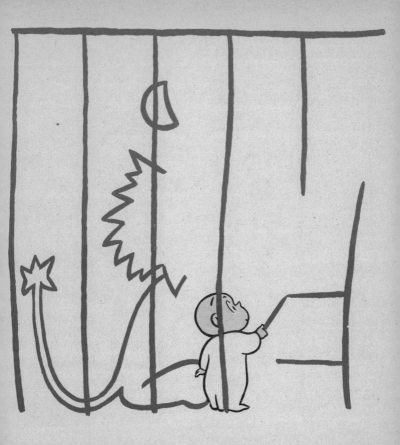

He got into the cage himself, with nothing
but a lion tamer's chair.

Then, like the bravest of lion tamers, he faced the lion.

With no thought of fear, he put his head right in the lion's mouth.

After he took his head out of the lion's
mouth it occurred to him that lions have
big teeth.

And, suddenly, he became a bit frightened
at how brave he had been.

But his own feelings didn't matter, Harold
told himself as he left the lion's cage.

The important thing at a circus is to make
the audience happy.

Harold saw that everybody in his audience wore a delighted smile.

Naturally, making so many people happy
made Harold happy.

And he smiled too as, very modestly,
he bowed.